WHERE EAGLES SOAR

A.G.Wayne Ezeard

T0156402

Trafford
PUBLISHING®

Order this book online at www.trafford.com
or email orders@trafford.com

Most Trafford titles are also available at major online book retailers.

© Copyright 2009 A. G. Wayne Ezeard.
All rights reserved. No part of this publication may be reproduced, stored in a retrieval system, or transmitted, in any form or by any means, electronic, mechanical, photocopying, recording, or otherwise, without the written prior permission of the author.

Note for Librarians: A cataloguing record for this book is available from Library and Archives Canada at www.collectionscanada.ca/amicus/index-e.html

Printed in Victoria, BC, Canada.

ISBN: 978-1-4269-0374-8 (sc)
ISBN: 978-1-4269-0376-2 (e-book)

We at Trafford believe that it is the responsibility of us all, as both individuals and corporations, to make choices that are environmentally and socially sound. You, in turn, are supporting this responsible conduct each time you purchase a Trafford book, or make use of our publishing services. To find out how you are helping, please visit www.trafford.com/responsiblepublishing.html

Our mission is to efficiently provide the world's finest, most comprehensive book publishing service, enabling every author to experience success. To find out how to publish your book, your way, and have it available worldwide, visit us online at www.trafford.com

Trafford rev. 6/25/2009

www.trafford.com

North America & International
toll-free: 1 888 232 4444 (USA & Canada)
phone: 250 383 6864 ♦ fax: 250 383 6804
email: info@trafford.com

For my wife Helen
Who has always been there for me,
and all of the adventures.

A collection of some of the poems and short stories that I have written over the past twenty years.

All the work here is a fictitious picture of events that have actually happened in this area over a period of time. So if some parts of this book seem familiar then maybe I've done some small means of justice in telling these tales. Otherwise any resemblance of any of my characters, to any person living or not is strictly coincidental.

Thank you to:
Studley Consulting for formatting and helping me find my way through the cyber-forest.
Don Pettit of Peace PhotoGraphics for the rodeo image.

Table of Contents

Living in God's Country

It's a cold full moon, the color of ice
As it gleams on a blanket of snow
And it's deadly as hell, if you're caught unaware
And it's well past forty below

It's quiet and still, not even a breeze
And the stars cast a silvery light
Even the coyote, buries deep in his lair
And waits out the worst of the night

Here in my cabin, with a fire in the hearth
I'm so thankful to God I'm inside
'Cause it's nature's way, to cull out the weak
And out there, tonight, something will die

What is it, about this place?
What hold does it have over man?
'Cause as much as I cuss it, and fight it
Oh, how I love it, it's a hell of a land

Yes, I've been in the south, I've played on the beach
I've been seduced by the sand and the surf
But it's here I'll stay, at least till I die
And if this damn cold don't kill me first

A. G. Wayne Ezeard

Autumn

Melancholy, haunting calls
Echo over pine clad hills
Leaves turning, brown and gold

Mating calls, blast the stillness of lone canyons
Where velvet rubbed, leaves tree trunks scarred
And sun rise warmth is hard to find

Shallow creek banks, skimmers of ice
Honking V's silhouette washed blue sky
The world is looking old

A. G. Wayne Ezeard (2001)

A Coffee Shop in Heaven?

Is there a coffee shop in Heaven?
A place for old Cowboys, like me and you
A gathering place, for old Partners
Some where we'd have some thing to do

We could reminisce about the stock sales
The poor price of beef, and the good horses we owned
And swap tales of places where we'd never been
Maybe talk about the wild seeds we had sown

I wonder if young Billy May is up there now?
He's the one who got him self drowned
When his horse floundered while we were crossing the river
We were trailing some beef into town

And then there's ol' Dad Tate,
who would drive the chuck wagon
Seems like for at least a hundred years
Man! He had a million jokes, he could keep you in stitches
You'd laugh till your eyes filled with tears

Oh it's a crazy thought I recon
As I puff on my pipe, in the old rockin' chair
And watch the colts playin' in the pasture
I'm thinking of old friends I hope to meet up there

Wow! a coffee shop in Heaven
Now there's one heck of a thought
I must have been kick'd in the head, one time to many
If that's some of the notions I got.

A. G. Wayne Ezeard

Too Much Fun

My ranching life is so much fun,
I chase my tail all day, getting things done
I get stompt on, shit on, kicked on, rained on
Pick my self off the ground a hundred times
My good wife laughs, asks me what the heck I'm doin
She thinks I'm out of my mind

Heel flies, nose flies, yes mosquitoes too
They'll drive you nuts if you let them get to you
Mud and manure all look the same
Run down your boots in the pourin' rain
Soaks your socks gets between your toes
Sticks in your ears, and gets up your nose

Hey now listen, I ain't one to bitch and complain
But I got another heifer stuck in the ditch again
Pulled her out just an hour ago
They ain't got no brains and it really shows
Got another calf to pull, the cows throwin' a fit
I gotta tell you, if I wasn't having so much fun, think I'd quit

A. G. Wayne Ezeard

Corra Leah

A.G. Wayne Ezeard

● CHAPTER 1

It was her laughter what got me first; one of those deep, rich, right from the heart, make you smile kind. Right off I knew I had to find out who that girl was.

Any way I go rip, tearin round the corner of the big wagon we used to haul the tourists on the hay rides, and oh my Lord there she was! Oh my! Yellow hair all gleamin' in the sun, biggest green eyes I ever seen, and those little freckles on her nose.

Fellas I was hit hard. Right there before me was the girl a man only dreams about, I didn't really think they actually got made that way. So when she looked over at me and smiled I thought I was gonna die, I just stood there all slack jawed, just staring like a total idiot, of course it didn't help any when I stepped back and tripped over the wagon tongue and fell into a pile of horse terds. Lordy, Lord it was a most humiliating moment indeed. A poor first impression on the girl I was gonna marry some day.

Boys I'm here to tell you the next few days I was mostly useless. Us workin' hands wasn't supposed to mix with the guests, but I was so busy tryin' to be where I could watch her the boss finally sent me off to ride fence till she left; probably a good thing.

"Hey Ben" a voice called out from the top bunk across the

room, that was Red my saddle partner. "You 'n me bin workin' this here place most of fifteen years, give or take. Where'd you ever meet a girl like that? Shure as shootin wasn't round here, and that's a fact."

"Your right about that ol' son, I admitted, but about eighteen, maybe twenty years ago I worked the Big Timbers Cattle and Guest Ranch, I was just a green kid then, and was hired on as season help, mostly a gopher hand. I was some glad to be shut of the place come end of season, there was absolutely no end to the ribbing I took from those guys I worked with.

Any way, you boys asked how come I never got hitched up and started my own spread, so now you know. Seems ever time I meet some nice gal I get to thinking about that yellow haired girl and I get all tongue tied and I develop lock jaw or some thing.

Hey its not like I ain't know'd a woman or two along the way, no siree Bob! Ever once in a while when I get a dollar or two, I some times get a notion and ride off down to the dance hall on the other side of town. Kind of a waste though, mostly I get so drunk I can't remember if I had a good time or not. But the girls always make me feel good when I first come through the door.

No, I'd sooner think on that pretty little yellow haired gal, Corra Leah. Corra Leah Kinkaid or something like that. I recon she's married up to some millionaire by now, livin' in some fancy place in the big city like she deserves.

But oh Lordy, I oughta be ashamed about some of the thoughts I have now and then.

● CHAPTER TWO

I heaved my self up from the edge of my bunk, and poured a cup of coffee from the old enamel pot that simmered on the back of the pot bellied stove that kept this old bunk house warm. A twelve by twenty foot shack with bunks six men, a table under the only window, where a poker game was goin on. Add a stove and a wood box by the door and you had what I'd called home for the past sixteen years or so. A pair of spurs, a worn out saddle, my boots worn down at the heels, two shirts patched at the elbows, and a fairly decent saddle horse was about all I had to my name, not much to show for a life time I suppose. Oh yes I had two hundred dollars hidden in a sock in the bottom of my saddle bags; but for the life of me I hadn't any idea what I was gonna do with it. Not enough to start my own place, and workin here was as good as any where, so I just stayed on.

Six feet tall, and built like a bean pole. My two front teeth busted off from a fight my last year of school when I was about fourteen, I got a face full of freckles big deep set eyes, a hawk nose what's been broke a time or two, and a perpetual cow lick right on the front of my head. No, I don't think any woman's gonna want to settle up with me, let alone that yellow haired gal any time soon. But it's shure nice to think about time and again."

"Hey Ben!" Red called. He startled me, as I must have dosed off for a moment.

"What?" I replied, no sense in ignoring him as I'd like to. I didn't really feel up to talking to anybody 'bout any thing at the moment, but I knew he'd keep at me till I did. He could be a total pain in the butt sometimes.

"Ben, I bin thinking on this Corra Leah you was talking

about, seems to me I should know her. She reminds me of a girl I went to school with, She was in the next grade up. I believe her daddy was a doctor or something. Ya shure, Dr.Matt Kinkaid; one of those tooth guys. Corra Leah, a real good lookin' blonde, real popular, was a cheer leader, went out with the quarter back I think. I hadn't thought 'bout her in years. I'll find out 'bout her for you if I can.

Oh great, just freakin' great. The guy who never, in all the years I knew him, said a dang thing about where he come from all of a sudden knows the only girl I could think about. The girl I had married a hundred times in my dreams. The mother of all my kids I'd never have. Crap! And this guy says he went to school with her.

This can't be so. She couldn't know somebody ordinary, specially a fella with the same job as me. It don't seem right some how. Lord, tell me this ain't real.

● CHAPTER THREE

Well, I gotta say the rest of the week just seem to drag by, I wish I'd kept my big mouth shut, I couldn't keep my mind on any thing, and the Boss chewed me out twice. Thank goodness it wasn't the busy part of the season. Most days it was just mendin' fence, checkin' water holes, regular stuff that always needed doin'. Come Saturday I was feelin' lower then a snake's belly in a wheel rut, and I was in a mind to go to town and get drunk as a billy goat. Maybe head down to the dance hall and stuff. Rip up the town a little. Even a hang over would feel better then this.

"Hey Ben! Wait up." It was Red ridin' up on a buckskin that I'd trade a month's wages for if he'd let him go. "Wash up ol' son" he says "we're cutting for town, let the wolf loose for a while. Somethin' I wanna show you" he said with a wicked grin on his face. Turns out I should have been payin' attention to that, however I was gonna go anyhow. So what the heck, why not?

Red was real tight lipped all the way in, just whistling a little tune with a silly smile on his face. Now this is a fella that can keep a conversation up for twenty minutes with a fence post, so a two hour ride to town with him like that should have made me nervous. But I was still brooding too much to pay attention.

"We'll stop at the bar first off, so's you can buy me a drink or two, Ben. Then I got a little surprise for you." Well I ain't much on surprises, but I was more than ready for a drink, and me having to pay wasn't a surprise at all.

After a couple of shots of cheap whisky, we sat at a table and ordered a beer, then Red up and asks me if I ever been over and visited the Ladies at the Little Canyon Dance Hall. "Good Lord Red!" As I choked on my beer, "No I ain't. You gotta talk about that kinda thing right out here in public! Jees Man. Besides, that place is a little to pricy for this cowboy. I go over to Bell's for those kinda things, she's a whole lot cheaper, and don't care how drunk you get, and long as you don't try'n bust the place up she won't throw you out till morning."

"Well it's your lucky day ol' Son. We're goin and I'm payin'. So what do you think about that?" he said.

"Your treat?" I mumbled. "Okay! But why do I have this feelin' I'm gonna regret this whole deal later on?" Red just give me that wicked grin again, and said "Drink up, you're gonna need it."

● CHAPTER FOUR

I never feel all that comfortable about going to those kind of places at the best of times. So I got to say I was a tad bit disappointed when we walked in. Not even close to what I imagined, for the kind of money Red dropped. Thirty bucks, wow. Actually it was kind of a seedy place I thought.

We were met at the door by a fairly heavy woman, with brassy blonde kind of hair, and too much greasy make up for me. She had pretty green eyes though, but I believe a lot of hard years must have been tough on her. Made me feel kind of sad and dirty.

"Ben, I want you to meet Corra Leah Kinkaid. Corra this here's Ben from the Dude Ranch you were at as a kid. He's still so in love with you he can't see straight."

"What!" I gasped. "No way, Red what kinda joke is this?" But there it was. That laugh, my God, it was her. Oh Lord, I had to sit down. I felt like I'd been sucker punched right in the gut. What a bloody joke on me. Corra Leah. The girl of my dreams; all these years only a two hour ride from the Ranch, and everybody's girl but mine. I needed a stiff drink. I had to get out of here.

"Hey, cowboy what's the matter Honey? Let's have a party, Corra Leah's gonna love you too. Come on I'll pour you a drink. Where you goin' any way?"

"I'd like to say it was nice to meet you" was all I could think of to say. I looked at Red and said "enjoy your evening. Hope you have a good laugh. Tell the boss I'll forward my address. Right now I'm gonna go get drunk. Then I think I'll go up to Beaver Lodge and buy me a little house. Maybe go to work for my cousin who owns a feed store there.

A. G. Wayne Ezeard

Tormented Wanderer

There's a lamp shining in a window, up there on yonder hill
And it seems to beckon, and haunt me
Though I know not who lives there
Yet it calls to me of times long past, and leaves me
Home sick for places I've never been

That lamp shining, there on yonder hill
A soft glow in the evening shadows
And it bares silent witness, as I bare my soul
To my troubled mind

That light shining through far off window
As a quail makes its final evening call
And the pines stand as silent sentries, haunting silhouettes
Against a cool night sky

There is a lamp far off on the horizon
It's not mine, nor ever will it be
For mine is the way of the wanderer, for ever wanting
But never can stand still,
But oh how it calls of times long past
And leaves me, home sick for places I've never been

A.G. Wayne Ezeard (1993)

The Price of Freedom

Written for Remembrance Day (Nov 2001)

Once more we gather to remember and pray
And give thanks to those who gallantly led the way
Yet Still! There are some who fail to understand
Freedom is purchased with blood on our hands.

History teaches, with war we win glory and fame
And says little about the carnage and pain
Or the widow who weeps, or the sons and daughters who die
While dictators, and war lords sit back on the side

It's gone on forever, since time first began
When greed and corruption spilled the first blood on the sand
The Roman's, the Nazis, and now Afghanistan
Oh Lord, please show your mercy on the innocent man

So let us remember all those who willingly go
And may God heal the scars on there conscience, and souls
Then let us pray for all of those who have died
And the widows, the mothers, and the children who cry

A. G. Wayne Ezeard (2001)

The Forgotten Soldier

In a chair, at the end of the hallway
Over looking the snow covered street
The old man sat patiently watching
As he did most nights of the week.

It was quiet in the dim lit hallway
On the second floor of that old hotel
Where it's worn carpets and faded paint
Left it with a musty smell

But it was home to the old Soldier
Whose family and friends had all but forgot
And if they remembered at all in passing
Rarely gave it a second thought

Pops was the only name every one called him
And if he had any other no one cared
He was just the old boy in room 212
With very little money to spare

Nobody knew where he came from
No one asked, and he never said
He'd just drink a little whisky in the evening
And polish the Medals that hung by his bed

What hair he had left was silver
There was character etched deep in his face
But no body knew the dreams that he dreamed
Or how he ended up in this place

They just found him there one morning
In the chair at the end of the hall
And they puzzled a bit over the smile on his face.
He'd answered the final call

A. G. Wayne Ezeard

Guitar Pickin' Cowboy

Just an ol' guitar pickin' cowboy
His hat pulled down over his eyes
A chew of Red Leaf under his lip
A Rodeo buckle he'd won, 1st prize

His boots were worn down at the heels
Wouldn't go 150 pounds soakin' wet
Nothin' about him at all special
Looked as down and out as they get

He strolled over to the stage and chuckled
"You boy's mind I sit in a while?"
He picked up my spare, checked the pitch,
Said "I'll try not to cramp yer style"

This guy had a touch all his own.
I just knew this was gonna be fun
So we played some Williams, and Skaggs,
And he knew all the runs

Then he reached over and finished my beer,
I called for another round
We played some Rock, some Rhythm and Blues,
And totally brought the house down

Then he sang a ballad, with a voice like crushed gravel
Came right from the guts you could tell
Then he nodded at Myles, said "Play me some fiddle."
Oh Man, you could see our chests swell

I'd never believed it if I hadn't been there.
This was as good as it ever would get
We never took a break till they closed down the bar
Then we played two more sets

It was a heck of a night, so we asked him to join us,
He smiled then he declined
Said he had his fill of the road and its empty promise
He just liked to sit in time to time

We wandered down to the café
And bought him some breakfast
Thanked him and found our way home
Heard he was killed a year or two later,
How it happened I've never known.

A.G. Wayne Ezeard

Charlie
A.G. Wayne Ezeard

● CHAPTER 1

It was 6:30 pm when Charlie turned off the road. The frozen
gravel crunched lightly under the pickup tires, headlights shining on icicle laden branches of the poplar trees that lined his
driveway.

"Good news folks!" The radio announced, "more rain
and wet snow, through out the night and all of tomorrow, ta-
pering off to intermittent showers and possible sunshine by
Sunday."

It was typical spring weather in the Peace Country, and
Charlie was glad the day was behind him. Cold, damp, and
tired he was happy to be home. Edith would have supper wait-
ing, some food, a hot shower, and Edith that's all he wanted at
the moment. Now, at 48 years old Charlie was easily contented
with the simple things in life. As he walked to the house the
smell of the farm was heavy in the air, and that was good too.

Edith met him at the door with a cup of coffee, and a kiss.
"How was your day love? Go have a shower and I'll dish up
supper, It's clam chowder, and garlic toast, your favorite." Every

thing was Charlie's favorite according to Edith, as she said that every time she announced the meal. Basically it was true as he liked most anything she fed him.

Over supper Edith, told Charlie all about her great day. Her favorite mare had foaled, and the filly was healthy, and had the same markings as her momma, but had the studs coloring: a real beauty for sure. So with the meal finished they donned there slickers, and with filled coffee cups they headed for the barn. Edith was right, the foal looked real nice, and another mare was showing signs; possibly tonight by the looks of it.

There's was a small place, a fifteen acre hobby farm, with a small barn, a wood shed , a chicken house, and a two bedroom trailer home. It wasn't much, but it was more then either had known since their childhood.

● CHAPTER 2

Charlie was the service manager at the local tire shop, and made a comfortable living. But it wasn't that many years ago he had nothing, or any one. Edith had changed all that when she came into his life six years earlier. Charlie some times thought God had finally got fed up and sent him a guardian Angel to keep him from his wild and crazy way. Some thing he was pretty grateful for.

This farm he had rented with a small loan from a very good friend. It had taken two years to pay that off, then finally he was able to secure a mortgage to buy the place. As it had been an estate deal it had came with some older farm equipment that was a bit rusty and in need of repair. That was okay because Charlie was good at that sort of thing.

Charlie had been born and raised here in this community, to a rather nice family

His parents were gone now, and his brother and sister had both moved away to the city years ago. Other than a Christmas card, he never heard from them. They had washed their hands of him long ago.

Edith had been left stranded in town; her husband had dropped her off at the laundry-mat while he supposedly went to have the car serviced. They had been traveling through, heading for the coast to make a fresh start. She never seen or heard from him again. And now eight years later she couldn't care less. She had Charlie, and for her, life had never been better. She believed herself blessed.

Life had not been kind to either of them, and they looked much older then Charlie's forty eight years, and Edith's fifty four but there was a quite dignity, and grace about them that gave an aura of peace and contentment; a look of victory over dark and violent times; a time that had left them battle scarred and weary, and no place to go but up.

Edith had been raised on a cattle ranch, but Charlie had lived his life in town. So any thing he knew about horses, he'd learned the hard way, through trial and error and hard work. It was something they both enjoyed and he wished he had discovered much earlier in life, It might have saved him a pile of grief over the years. But there was no sense crying over it now, done was done. He knew you gained nothing by looking back, and life wasn't no place for quitters.

● CHAPTER THREE

At one time Charlie had been a good looking guy while he was in school, he was easy going and full of fun and mischief, the life of the party. Everyone's friend. And with his two best buds, Tim and John, they were the original three musketeers, where one was, so were the rest. As youngsters they played ball and hockey and dreamed up the craziest stunts. Getting caught skinny dipping at the local swimming hole by the minister's daughter was more than enough to earn them lots of fame. And attention, especially from fathers who still believed in corporal punishment. Actually they were pretty good boys. And Charlie was a pretty good athlete at that time, kind of handy to have on a team. John who excelled at hockey was the quieter one; the 'A' student. Tim was the all round athlete, star quarter back, and a mean pitcher, he was the hero all through high school.

Tim's dad owned a construction company, and had the money to send him to hockey camp and such things the rest of the boys couldn't afford. All though he had to work for it any spare time he had. So he wasn't exactly spoiled, his dad wanted him to learn the business and take it over one day. There was no doubt about his future, he was going to be a carpenter, and business owner one day and that was a given. Had some one bothered to ask Tim about it they would have heard a different story. But no one did. And so as Tim went into his senior year he got somewhat belligerent and miserable to be around, week ends were spent partying.

Forgetting to show up for practice, get completely drunk Saturday night, and spend Sunday sick and hung over. Tim could get a 'C' plus with out even trying, and a carpenter didn't need a degree any way, so why bother.

John was a different guy altogether, he had to work hard for every mark, and everything he got. His dad was a mechanic at the automotive dealer ship, and John worked there after school, washing cars and cleaning up. The rest of his time other than the Saturday game was spent cramming the books. As he got older he spent less time with Charlie and Tim. He didn't enjoy their antics anymore, and was more apt to spend Saturday night watching the game or going to the movies with his girl friend.

Charlie, on the other hand was the amiable sort. Always ready to lend a hand or pitch in and help where ever needed, every one liked him. His father worked shift work at the mill, so was not always around. Charlie did all right in school when he actually applied himself, but would sooner skip out and go fishing, or take a day job for spending money. Anytime there was a party you could count on Tim, and Charlie to show up. Tim would get drunk and stoned then pass out, and Charlie would be sneaking out the back door with someone's girl friend.

● CHAPTER FOUR

At the age of fifteen, Charlie was sure he had all the answers, and was quite convinced there had to be more to life then just going to School every day, he was completely bored and frustrated with the whole concept. Charlie had a vivid imagination that never seemed to stop and the more his father rode him about his grades and his lack of scholastic interest the worse he got and the more time he spent doing other things and hardly ever went home, unless his dad was on night shift. Charlie's step mother rarely paid much attention to him. So

when the circus came to town in May, Charlie took the oppor-
tunity to get employment as a ride operator and left town with
them, he had a marvelous time with them for about six months,
then got tired of the long days and quit. Only a jerk would stay
at that stupid job he would tell any one who would listen. Your
day started at eight in the morning, work until midnight, seven
days a week then tear everything down, drive all night, then set
it all back up again. Work your butt off in all kinds of weather
for very little money. Only an idiot would stay at some thing
like that. Fact of the matter was he'd been fired for goofing off
and his poor attitude towards work. Charlie went back home
for the lack of a better plan.

Things didn't change much over the next little while, he
went to some parties but they were kind of a drag, with every one talking school and sports it was getting boring. There
wasn't much to do through the day, every one was either in
school or working, so no one to hang with. He could probably
get a job at the mill or some thing, but that was for losers, he
was his own man. The fact that he was broke didn't seem to
motivate, or concern him. He could always con some one into
paying his way. He'd find some thing to do when he was ready.
He finally got a job at the local filling station, pump gas, fix
tires, clean the floors, that lasted a week and then he got fired.
It didn't matter; the boss was a jerk any way. So who cared?

New Year's day would for ever be a land mark in his mind.
His father booted him out of the house, told him he wasn't supporting a bum any more. And until he got a change of attitude don't bother coming back. Screw them all he thought I
don't need them, or anyone. It was later that week when he
left town with a group of kids in an old V.W. mini bus heading for Vancouver. Life was going to be a whole lot better there

and a lot warmer too. Charlie had no idea what he would do when he got there, nor was he worried about it. Charlie was the total care free optimist. He'd find some thing to do. So when everyone's money was gone and there was no more gas for the van, or food to be had, he got a job at a gas station fixing tires, pumping gas and stuff. The fact he'd had the same job making fifty cents an hour more about six moths ago had no bearing on anything, heck this was just a lark till he found some thing else to do. Three months later he was let go for showing up late, and poor attitude. He took a job washing dishes at the corner Diner. It wasn't permanent, only till he found some thing better. He wasn't going to take any hand outs from no one, he would make his own way. It wasn't long until he had a good paying job driving a delivery truck around the city. Great money weekends to himself, what could be better. Two pay cheques later Charlie was looking for a new line of work. He couldn't get up in the morning because he liked to party hard every night; heck that job was for losers any way. He didn't need it.

By the time Charlie was Twenty years old, he'd had thirty jobs, and as many address's. He didn't care, he was having a ball. He'd been to the Calgary Stampede, Had hitched a ride and worked for two weeks at the Canadian National Exhibition in Toronto, and had been stoned for three days at a Rock fest in some place called Woodstock. It was along about then Charlie got awful sick, and spent a week in the Hospital. He had contracted Hepatitis, and Gonorrhea. He was lucky he was cured. But he was back on the streets again, broke, no work, kicked out of his room cause he didn't pay his rent.

Charlie got another job in a clothing factory. He vowed this was it, he was going to settle down, quit his rowdy ways, save his money and get a nice apartment, and buy a car. His next pay cheque he bought an old pick up truck, and his next cheque had his separation slip with it. Charlie never seemed to learn. He could never figure out why every one else got all the luck. Why was the world against him?

It wasn't his fault. No one had explained to Charlie that you had to show up on time a work hard to keep a job. No one liked a lousy attitude, and the world didn't owe him a living.

● CHAPTER FIVE

Charlie returned home when he was twenty three. After all this time drifting around the country, it would be great, a lot of fun. He was looking forward to sitting around with the guys, telling them all about his wild experiences, having a few laughs. Heck hadn't been to many people seen, or done all the things he had. He'd be the home town hero. Charlie was driving an old car he'd bought for a hundred dollars, and still had seventy five more in his pocket so he would be fine for a few days, then he was going to get that real good job he'd always dreamed of, find a little house and show his old man, and this town, Charlie was a force to be reckoned with; a man of experience. They would be lucky to have him.

A week later he was working at the mill; his job was on the hot pond, walking up and down the cat walk guiding the logs onto the conveyor chain with a long pole with a cantle on the end. It was outside work and cold in the winter time, but he didn't care it was just a means to get by till he found some thing more suitable; a job that paid real money. He certainly deserved better than this.

Charlie had a dream of some kind of executive position. Where you came to work at nine, took an hour or so for lunch, and went home at four, and never work week ends. He had no idea where, or what that job would be, or what kind of qualifications he would need. Nor did he care at the moment, he was much to busy with his social life. There were parties to go to, girls to chase, he was having a ball.

Charlie got fired with in two months, of course the way he told it the foreman didn't like him, and was looking for an excuse so his son could have the job. That place was for losers any way, he didn't need it. One thing about Charlie he always had a ready excuse. After all, as a victim of circumstance, he didn't have any good luck.

Charlie got hired on down at the Turbo Gas Bar and Car Wash, on the afternoon shift, three to eleven with Saturday off, even though it paid a dollar an hour less he didn't care, at least he was having fun. And when the boss left at six, it was just him and the cashier girl, and a couple of school kids. He was having a ball. The cashier was going out with him, and the guys seemed impressed with the stories he'd tell of his adventures, he liked to spice them up a bit to make them more exciting, he figured these morons would never know the difference anyway.

Cindy Lou was the cashiers name, and surprise, surprise! Cindy Lou was pregnant. Charlie was going to be a dad. Wow; this was great, he was making three, seventy five an hour. He'd just go find an apartment and look after every thing. He always wanted to be a dad.

● CHAPTER SIX

Charlie was down town the next day after the news of the baby, when he ran into his old friend John. It was the first time he'd seen him since he got home. John was in cover alls, and had some grease on his hands and chin, and that big grin he always wore. "Hey Charlie, how the heck are you doing? Haven't seen you in a long time, where you been?" He asked.

Charlie explained he was back and was the assistant manager down at the Turbo.

Charlie never liked people to think he wasn't on top. "What are you doing with yourself John, I'm glad to see you" he said.

John was still working down at the car dealership, and had his mechanics license now. He and Donna were married, and living in a small apartment over the hardware store. Jesus, Charlie thought, what a chump! John, who stayed in school, never went anywhere, and now he was living over a store. He is probably no better off than I am. I've got a baby coming, and a job, and I've been all over the country.

Charlie sold his old car for fifty bucks and rented an old three room house behind the moving and storage company place. It wasn't much, but it would do until he and Cindy got on their feet. Cindy's mom and dad tried desperately to talk her into staying at home, and they would help her. But she moved in with Charlie and in a few weeks Charlie had a major problem on his hands. Cindy was having a hard time with her pregnancy, and had to quit work.

Charlie had no medical insurance to pay the doctors. Charlie was fired for stealing money from the carwash. No charges were laid, as nothing could be proved. He told Cindy he was fired, after he told his boss off, because he wouldn't stay off his back. Charlie still couldn't accept responsibility for his own actions. After all, he was a victim of circumstance.

Charlie got lucky again. Charlie always got lucky. He got a job at the tire shop fixing flats and mounting tires. He was very good at it and was promoted to a service truck. He went out on the road fixing tires on transports and farmers tractors. Heck, he was even making good money for a change. It was hard work, but it was great, and in a few months he got a raise. By the time Cindy had her baby, he had saved enough money to buy baby furniture and fixings. He even had a car, a good one that the finance company helped him buy. All he had to do was make a payment every month, just like paying the rent. Every Saturday they closed at 4 o'clock. Charlie and the boys would go down for a beer or two and watch the strippers for awhile.

Then he'd take Kentucky Fried Chicken home for a treat. Cindy always got mad at him for spending the money on beer but what the heck, he worked hard all week and he figured he deserved it. Not all men brought home a steady cheque every week. Cindy, didn't hardly deserve him sometimes, Charlie thought!

It was getting to a point where Charlie was going to the bar twice a week, for lunch as well. He'd have a burger and a beer.

Watching the peelers helped him take his mind off the rat race for an hour. It was his lunch hour, and it wasn't any of the boss's business what he did with it. Just because he was driving a company truck, didn't mean he couldn't have a few beer during the day. It was one of those days when he was just heading in the bar for lunch, when he spotted his old friend John going in the cafe up the street. He was all dressed up nice, and was with some other gentlemen in suits. 'That's weird', thought Charlie, 'What would John be doing with those guys?' He was just a mechanic. Must be a funeral or something like that. He'd have to ask him the next time he saw him.

A week later, Charlie was called to go down to the car dealership to switch over some tires on a truck. When he inquired about John, he was told that John was the service manager at the new Chevy dealership across town. 'Holy shit!' thought Charlie, 'Some guys get all the breaks! How come him, and not me? I could do that. What did John know that he didn't?' Charlie brooded about that all day. That night he went straight to the bar and got pretty drunk. In fact, he got so drunk, that Cindy had to phone in sick for him the next day.

Charlie started hitting the bottle pretty regularly after that and he and Cindy were fighting a lot. He was missing more days from work, and was issued a warning slip. Who the hell did those guys think they were? They couldn't do without him. He was about the best thing that ever hit that place. If he was gone they'd be sorry. A lot of customers liked him and they'd probably not deal with the store again if he left.

He got home very late Thursday night, and there was a note on the table. Cindy had taken the baby and left him. Who cared! He was better off without her anyway. She was a weight around his neck. She was holding him back. It was all her fault. He was stuck with this dead-end job, and he didn't need it or her.

● CHAPTER SEVEN

Life started heading downhill for Charlie pretty quickly with Cindy gone, and it wasn't long until he was fired from his job. "You're a good worker, Charlie", his boss told him, "but we can't tolerate your tardiness anymore. When you clean up your act and get your problems, whatever they are, straightened out, come back and see us. Maybe we can find room for you again!" That's just exactly what Charlie needed to hear -- the company couldn't do without him.

They were just giving him a holiday. Well, he could use one, he thought. A few days later, he was sitting in the cafe, having breakfast about noon, when in came his old friend John, all dressed up in a suit and tie. "Hey John, come on over here and visit with me," Charlie yelled! "I haven't seen you in about two years now. How is that fancy job as service manager working out for you?"

"Well Charlie", John said, "I'm no longer a service manager. I spent a year and a half doing that job. Then I took some up-grading courses at night, learned computer fundamentals, took a minor business management course and I'm now general sales, manager and consultant for the mill here in town. How about you, Charlie?" John asked.

"Oh, me? Hell I'm just given' her!" Charlie replied. "I'm the assistant manager down at the tire shop now. I'm on holidays at the moment."

"Hey, that's great man!" John said. "How about your family?"

"Well, Cindy hasn't been feeling too good lately, so her and the kid have been staying with her folks until she's better. We'll have to get together when she gets back! We'll have you guys over for supper."

"That's fine," John said, "We'll look forward to that."

They said their goodbyes, and John picked up the tab. When he left, he waited at the corner and watched sadly as Charlie disappeared up the street and into the bar.

God, how could Charlie tell him stories like that? John had been sort of keeping an eye on Charlie, hoping his old friend was on his way in life so he knew that Charlie had lost his job, and his family had left him. He didn't have heart to tell Charlie that their childhood pal, Tim, had overdosed on drugs and died. His body was being flown home, and the funeral was next Friday. He hated the thought of going, but he guessed he better.

No one had heard anything from Tim for over three years, ever since he had got all doped up at a party, broke up the furniture in the house, and smashed his car into the wall of the restaurant. His old man had given him a bunch of money, told him to get the hell out of town for awhile and get him self straightened out. Well, his homecoming was not exactly what anyone was looking forward to, to but at the same time, no-one was surprised.

'Shit', John Forward thought, 'How do you just up and forget all about your childhood pals? Tim dead, and Charlie was not really all that much better off.' How is it possible for a person to pick himself up from the bottom of the pile and proceed to go down hill even further? I don't know, but Charlie managed it. Oh, it was no rapid thing, just a slow deterioration, a total embarrassment to all who knew him. In fact, most of those who knew him avoided him. When Cindy finally married a nice guy, who worked at the mill, everyone conveniently forgot to tell Charlie, as he would just be too drunk anyway. Charlie and Cindy had never been legally married. Cindy had been smart enough to give their child her family name. So nothing was wrong, in fact for Cindy Lou, everything was just right for a change. Oh, Charlie had managed to find out about Tim, and make it to his funeral, but, other than that, nothing. Oh, the world kept turning, things were changing, but not for Charlie.

His unemployment ran out and he took a job as a waiter in the hotel. He got fired the third day for drinking on the job, so he stayed drunk for a week.

When he sobered up, he realized he was in trouble so he resolved to go home and clean up and get back to work. Over the next five years Charlie had a dozen different jobs. He drove tow truck, taxi, and skidder. He pumped gas, washed dishes and tried selling vacuum cleaners. Each job would last long enough for him to get a grub stake, then he'd hit the bottle and get run off his job. It wasn't long before Charlie had exhausted his supply of places to work. The only ones who would hire him were just day jobs - unloading a truck, delivering flyers - that sort of thing.

His mother died, and his father didn't even want him at the funeral. That was the last straw. Charlie was totally insulted now! How dare his father treat him that way? He was a decent person, who never hurt anyone in his life. Didn't anyone realize he was a victim of circumstances beyond his control. To hell with them all!

He was going to blow this town. Enough was enough. At thirty-six years old, he'd given this town all he was going to. He figured if he could make five hundred dollars, he would have enough money to go to Calgary and get a good job, start over. So Charlie convinced the service station to hire him back again for the third time. The problem was Charlie's drinking buddies always knew when Charlie was working and had money.

The first payday, Charlie managed to avoid them and even banked half his pay. It was hard to do, but he also moved out of the hotel room he had rented and moved into a basement apartment; actually, just a sitting room with fridge and stove. The sink was in the bathroom. Charlie actually didn't look too bad with a haircut and new clothes. He was still a tad shaky, and the cold really bothered him, but he was confident he had things under control. In reality, his boss was pleasantly surprised. Although a bit suspicious, he was supportive too and like most people, he actually liked Charlie. Charlie had a winning personality and in all his drunken stupors, he had managed to remain civil and was not obnoxious. He was welcome most anywhere.

The next payday arrived and Charlie went to his employer to announce he was quitting and moving away someplace where no one knew him. So it would be easier for him to straighten out his life.

His boss, a man not much older than himself, explained to Charlie that it wasn't necessary. That his friends were right here! They would help him, if he would just let them. But, when Charlie made up his mind, or better still, when he got a bright idea, then that's what he did, regardless. So, with that in mind, Charlie cashed his

Pay cheque, withdrew his savings, and bought a bus ticket for Calgary. He got himself a suitcase and a new change of clothes. Then Charlie did what was typical of a victim of circumstance; he went to the bar to say goodbye to his pals.

● CHAPTER EIGHT

For the first time in his life, Charlie was in trouble. He was in jail. What happened, he wasn't sure. Apparently, someone kept harping at him to loan them some money, and got a little over-insistent. Charlie, who was more than just a little bit drunk, got violent. Charlie, who was only going to have a couple of beer, didn't realize he was at that point of saturation that that was all it took to get him bombed. For the first time in his life, human resources helped him out.

They arranged his bail, gave him some eating money and some friendly advice. Charlie went straight down to the bar to see what happened to his wallet, all his money, his bus ticket and his suitcase. The bouncer met him at the door, refused to let him in, threatened to have the cops come and get him again. He didn't know anything about a suitcase or money. His last words stung Charlie pretty deep. "You're just another lousy stinkin' drunk. Where the hell do you get off accusing anyone of stealing anything from you? You don't got nothin' worth stealin'."

That hurt and Charlie brooded about that for awhile. It really bothered him. He was walking down the street when he met his old friend John. Upon inquiring how Charlie was doing, John was told all about his ordeal and how wrongly he had been used. John just shook his head and wished Charlie luck. Then he walked away in disgust. 'Screw you,' thought Charlie, 'you're lucky you got a good job. What do you know about having rotten luck all your life? He wasn't a victim of circumstance. What would John know? He had a wife that helped him -- probably kissed somebody's ass to get that good job anyhow. Screw him. Screw them all - they could go to hell.'

Charlie's court date arrived, and Charlie appeared before the judge charged with public mischief and property damage. He was fined one hundred dollars and told to stay out of that particular bar for a period of one year.

Welfare was now a way of life for Charlie. Drunken binges, small amounts of food, and if he brought a bottle of wine, he was usually welcome in someone's place, where he'd usually wake up in the morning.

Charlie didn't know what day was what anymore, nor did he care. He got his welfare cheque. He cashed it and spent it. No one really even recognized him anymore, nor did they care.

Charlie was forty-two years old, when one morning he woke up in an alley; another first for Charlie. His coat and boots were gone. So was his money, and what was left of any dignity he might have still had. Charlie had been rolled, literally beaten up and robbed. By the looks and feel of things, probably even more things had been done to him. Charlie leaned against the wall and cried -- soundless tears at first, then totally uncontrollable sobs. His body hurt and he couldn't stop shaking. His head was a dull roar. His bowels had voided, and he stunk; a total wreck, a complete waste of a human being. Charlie had always stood six foot and weighed around two hundred pounds. He wouldn't go one hundred and forty pounds right now. Charlie stayed there for quite awhile, trying to get himself oriented. When he stood up and tried to walk, he screamed and fainted.

It was three days later when Charlie woke up. He stared around at totally unfamiliar surroundings. He was strapped down, and couldn't move. Even his hands were bound. What the hell was going on any way? Who was this lady?

"Good morning, sir. I see you're finally awake. That's good," she said. "The doctor will be in to see you shortly." Then she quietly left. For over an hour, Charlie pondered what happened to him. What was he doing in the hospital? Why was he tied down? What had happened?

The doctor, a young friendly but tired looking man, came in. After a few minutes of the usual blood pressure test, check the eyeballs and feel the pulse routine, he asked Charlie if he had any idea where he was, or why. Well, Charlie knew where he was, but not the why.

Charlie had been brought in by ambulance, late at night, when he'd been discovered in an alley. He had three broken ribs, was suffering from exposure, malnutrition and the D.T.'s. There was no real need to keep him in the hospital any longer. There was nothing they could do for him. He could come back in a few weeks and have the bandages removed. The doctor recommended Charlie get some proper food into him, and be careful. Then, he bade Charlie goodbye. There were more serious cases to look after. A shortage of beds didn't leave enough time, or room to worry too much about some hopeless idiot, who was only going to drink himself to death.

Charlie's first stop was at the welfare office where, after he explained his case, they gave him enough money to see him through to his next regular cheque. With a new suit of clothes, a haircut, shave, and bath, Charlie did the hardest thing he had ever done. He actually asked for help.

He phoned his old friend John. While definitely reluctant, John agreed to meet with Charlie. "Charlie, I don't know why, but, yes I'll help you; but, only if you agree to help yourself," John said. "Donna told me to bring you home. You can sleep in the spare room tonight. Then, tomorrow we'll talk some more. It's Friday, so I have a couple days off. I'll do what I can, but, so help me God, Charlie, if you screw up, or let me down, you'll wish you were back in that alley. My family doesn't need this, and I'm equally sure I'll regret it as well. You asked for help, and that's a step in the right direction. I couldn't face myself in the mirror if I turned my back."

For the first time ever, Charlie didn't pat himself on the back for bailing himself out of another situation. Charlie felt lower than a snake's belly in a wheel rut. Laying in bed that night, Charlie realized what a complete jerk he had been all these years. It had been ages since he'd had a woman to lay beside. Booze had robbed him of his strength, youth, virility, and most of his productive years. How stupid could he be!

A childhood prayer kept going through his head, as he drifted off to sleep.

No one bothered him and he slept late the next day.Donna made him coffee and breakfast, and when he was done he showered and changed into some old clothes of John's.They were comfortable and warm. Donna poured him more coffee, and then she started into him. Reminding him of his total failure, she climbed up one side of him and down the other. When she was done, she said "What the hell have you got to say for yourself Charlie?"

Charlie, who hadn't been able to look at her in the eye from the beginning, simply said "Donna, how do I apologize to the whole world for the jerk I've been? But, I promise you this. I've picked myself up off the garbage heap, and I'm going to do something with myself."

"Have you never had a goal Charlie, anything you really wanted to accomplish in your life?" Donna asked. Charlie thought about that for awhile, and then admitted, not a thing he could think of.

"Well!" Donna said, "That's most of your problem. If you don't have a goal, then how do you figure you'll ever get anywhere? A ship never leaves port unless it has a planned route, does it? A plane never leaves the ground without first filing a flight plan! A person with no interests or goals is as lost as a plane would be if the pilot knew not where he was going, or how to read the instruments to guide him there."

Monday morning, Charlie joined A.A. He went to the unemployment office and checked out job training programs. He got his next welfare cheque and told the lady he would never be back for another one. She wished him well.

He gave Donna a hundred dollars, and she agreed he could stay, providing he stayed with A.A., talked to them when it started going bad for him, and as soon as he found a job, he had to move out. Charlie agreed.

Charlie stayed with John and Donna for six weeks. Between A.A. meetings and church on Sunday, combined with good meals and some physical exercise, he was feeling better and putting on some weight. It was at the A.A. meetings that he learned of the single's club that held a weekly dance, with no booze allowed. Charlie joined, and found some good friends who were more than familiar with his story.

Charlie was learning fast that it was hard to change, but he could do it with the right friends. He realized that with no goal in his mind, he was lost. Without the proper education, a person had no chance to progress, and to stand still in life, was to wither and die like the roses in winter. He knew that there was no first mate to take the helm. You have to be the captain of your own ship. He was nothing without faith and love. You have to take control over your own destiny and have the courage to stand up and make things happen when the going gets tough.

The only place you could get this ability, was within yourself. No one needs a loser, and winners are contagious. People are attracted to them.

Charlie met Edith one night at a dance, and the attraction was mutual. Charlie had gone back to work at the tire store, in customer service. He was good at that, and the store owner was more than ready to lend a hand to help Charlie.

Like many people, he just needed to be asked. It's amazing

what people are willing to do for you, if you just ask, and they realize you are genuine and honest.

Charlie and Edith moved into a bedsitting room a couple of months later. It was a match that worked well. Charlie needed attention and reassurance, and Edith needed someone to pamper and mother. One Saturday evening in June, Charlie and Edith were driving around the countryside taking in the sights, when they spotted a small farm. 'For Sale or Lease', the sign read. The place was vacant, and after an hour of exploring the premises, they both realized this is what they wanted. This was the next goal.

It was a month later that Charlie approached John and Donna with the idea of a small hobby farm, where he might raise saddle horses. Donna was totally enthusiastic about the idea and they agreed to finance Charlie, for two thousand dollars for two years, to get him started.

It took a while, and a lot of work, but over a few years they had fixed up the place real nice. Edith loved gardening and flowers, so it kept her busy.

The next six years were very hard, but enjoyable. And finally now after so many miss spent years Charlie had been promoted to service manager, and their horse herd had increased to seven mares and one stud. All the young stuff was halter broke, and sold at auctions when they were yearlings. It was not a real money-making proposition, but they didn't care. It was a hobby that they both understood and loved.

"Come on up to the house, Charlie! We'll have another cup of coffee, and I'll beat your pants off at a game of crib, eh?" Charlie grinned, and slipped his arm around Edith and said, "You'll never see the day you can beat my pants off at anything, Lady."

Resume From a Wrangler

To The Commercial Bank
Most Any Town

G.W. Peabody
Mountain of Debt Ranch
Box 2, Broke Flat Mountain

To the Hiring Boss,

I respectfully submit my résumé
I believe you'll find it pretty good
You'll find I'm a fair hand at most any thing
So I thought you should find a spot for me if you could.

I'm real good at spottin' a sucker, or a con
So I'm thinking a loans officer might be a good spot
And heck I all ready know all the procedures
Cause of all the loans I got

I know all about horses, and cattle
Their pedigree, their value and stuff
And don't worry bout any them slow players
Cause I know how to be tuff

Why just ask my friend Luke, he owed me twenty bucks
And hadn't paid me in most a year
So we arm wrassled, double or nothing
He won. So now were clear

I figger if I work real hard.
Some thing I should have done long ago
I can pay up all my over due notes, and get back to ranchin'
May be I could make another ten years or so.

A. G. Wayne Ezeard (1996)

Dad

He gets up a little later now than he used to
His movement a little more painstaking and slow
He coughs up some crud and spits in the can
And puts the coffee to boil on the stove

Oh his mind is still sharp and his vision is fair
Though he works with trembling hands
He looks at her picture that hangs on the wall
Then cracks two eggs in the pan

There's not much to do, the cattle's long gone
The biggest chore is just lookin after him self
And he thinks for a moment, what the Dickens is there left
As he takes the bread down from the shelf

Why just light years ago, he was young and in love
Not a thing he wasn't willing to do
But now the kids are grown and gone, Mom's passed on
And father time is catching up with him to

There's a creak and a groan as a gate swings in the wind
He should fix it but what the heck for
The trees and the weeds are taking over the fields
And he can't work them himself any more

Oh, there's the barn, and the tractor, the hay shed and plow
Things to remind him of good times gone by
But with the high cost of farming his kids can't take over
It would bankrupt them even to try

This good life is gone, you can't afford to compete
There's another farm sale just down the road
And the end of an era is right here in sight
And it's leaving him feeling empty and old

A. G. Wayne Ezeard

The Hands of Time

Down lone canyons in my mind
Through the stumbling blocks of time
In cobwebbed crevices I find
Those magic moments that were mine

Back to child hood is where I go
A time of sun, and surf, and falling snow
When time was a thing that moved so slow
And there were the most exciting things to show

Of school yard fights, and baseball games
And grownups with the silliest names
Or getting soaked in pouring rains
And some one always there to heal your pain

Of course nothings ever as it seemed
We were always much faster and brighter in our dreams
And we may not be the person we could have been
I'm sure of course, you know what I mean

Like your first date, who held your hand so tight
You would just die if she couldn't go with you
on Saturday night
And now, all though I try as hard as I might
I can't remember for the life of me what she looked like

A. G. Wayne Ezeard (1990)

A Bull Called Rock and Roll

We had the bull in the chute,
He was a Hell of a brute
He was born without a soul
And he was mean as sin
When we hazed him in
We called him Rock and Roll

Cowboys came from far and wide,
Paid their money to make the ride
And none prepared to eat some dirt
Eighteen hundred pounds of mean,
Ugliest critter we'd ever seen
No one got killed, but most were hurt

He would jackknife, spin, twist both ends,
Find new places he could bend
He'd knock them clean out cold
Cowboys howled cowboys cried,
Some was sure they was gonna die
On this Bull called Rock and Roll

Extra clowns were ushered in,
Just to try and corner him
While cowboys gained their feet.
Seven gates and a corner post,
Were crumbled up and looked like toast
There wasn't a soul left in their seat

The smell of blood, and dust, and gore,
The Bull was racking up the score
No one stood a chance
Then one poor cowboy cried in vain,
I'm gonna try him once again
Soon as I change my pants

The crowd was wild as could be,
No one sat including me
And I'll remember till I'm old
When a little girl bout nine years old,
Slipped a ring into his nose
And quietly led out that Bull, called Rock and Roll

A.G. Wayne Ezeard

The Auctioneer

I sat in the bleachers overlooking the crowd
But I had my eyes on the man in the ring
It was kind of fun to watch, 'cause as casual as he seemed
He never missed a thing

He knew the buyers and he watched them close
It was a pleasure to watch him ply his art
The cattle came through in singles and groups
And each man doing his part

A sense of excitement hung in the air
It wasn't any thing you could touch, or could feel
But as the sun rays broke through the dust in the room
The smells from the stock pens made it all real

She's seven hundred pounds boys, who'll gimme 99
Now it's a dollar, who'll give a dollar one
The bidding goes on till every things sold
Another day at the market is done

The auctioneer and the rancher
There sort of partners, in a game with the bank
And its there in the ring where it all comes together
And we all have the buyers to thank

Yup! A whole years work, will your goals be realized
Or do they all go up in smoke
It's a game where the action is fun, and hard work
And we all live on courage and hope.

A. G. Wayne Ezeard

A '48 Ford

The feeling of wealth can be exhilarating and fun
The just rewards of a job well done
A new suit of clothes, a night on the town
Your wife and daughters in new silken gowns

A new car to drive, a home on the lake
Money in the bank, more deals to make
Then out of nowhere, for no reason at all
A small voice in your mind starts to beckon and call

Then you think of the days oh so long ago
Hide the girls in the back off to the drive in you'd go
Two bucks worth of gas and a six pack of beer
Roaming the back roads without any fear

Oh, Man, a 48 Ford, the big flat head V8
Steering was tricky, not much for brakes
Tires were bald, only two rusted hub caps
The floor boards were gone, it was painted flat black

Yah! Those days are long gone
And my hair is showing some gray
But I'll feel a whole lot younger
When I find another 48 Ford someday

03.G. Wayne Ezeard

God's Gracious Wonder

Oh let these eyes look and see, all the Gifts God's given me
As I look out upon my horizons
And I'm constantly amazed, at the world He's made
And no money need I pay for this splendor

As I watch wild geese careen along wheat fields, and streams
And disappear into the wild blue yonder
I'm humbled and I'm proud to realize I've been allowed
To be part of His gracious wonder

When the sun kisses goodbye to the crimson sky
And the evening star points its finger
I watch a hawk sail down and catch its prey on the ground
I bow my head, in thanks for all this splendor

As the seasons roll around and his blessings abound
I marvel at His creation
These gifts have been given to everyone under His Heaven
And to each and every nation

A.G. Wayne Ezeard

Where Eagles Soar
A.G. Wayne Ezeard

● CHAPTER ONE

I was fifteen miles shy of Buffalo Creek, heading for home.

Fifteen miles of rough rugged country; a land of trees, rocks, and creeks that would be running wild over their banks in the spring of the year, but now were no more than a trickle among the boulders that lined the bed. Boulders worn smooth from who knows how many years of water pounding down out of those rugged wind ravaged foothills I had just left behind me.

In the summer this place would be hot and dry, home for the

wild game that sought shelter beneath the poplars and spruce that inhabited the area, although often opening into large natural meadows that were laced with bluebells, wild rose, and fireweed that grew amongst the wild grasses. There were many such places in this country, each looking the same yet different in their own way. The sort of land a man never got tired of looking at no matter what the season although winter would find these trails choked with snow and ice, making them treacherous if not impossible to travel.

Now late in October as I rode half dozing in the saddle, the poplars were as old men with their branches naked, soaking up the afternoon sun of an Indian Summer knowing the icy grip of winter was only around the corner.

High over head an eagle swooped and soared, flaunting his freedom among the clouds, leaving only the wind singing softly through the spruce boughs.

It would be great to be home, I'd been gone about twelve days now, lazing around up in the Stewart Lake area, just taking a few days off, doing a little hunting and sightseeing, relaxing after a hard summer on the ranch.

My home, the Diamond E Ranch, lies about twelve miles west of town and straddles Buffalo Creek. The homestead sits on a big bend in the river, protected by a spruce covered hill on the north and east sides, giving us a good south westerly exposure, a good place to run cattle.

Now I admit calling it a ranch is being a bit over zealous. We're sort of small potatoes compared with some in the area. But she's mine, bought and paid for; a half section of good land with log built home, barns, and corrals and a government lease on another section adjoining to the west. The only home I'd known since I quit my wandering ways.

I was riding a little sorrel gelding that I just broke this fall, a pretty thing with three white socks and a matching blaze on his face. I was trailing old Rebel as a back up and packhorse. Ol' Reb had been on my string about six years now and a steadier horse never found.

If I'd been riding Reb at this time I might not have got into the jack pot I stumbled into so sudden. But hindsight is like hind tit, I say, not worth a shit. Horses and bears are like matches and dynamite, pure hell when it meets unexpected.

Hell, I didn't mean to drop in unexpected for lunch or anything, but that ol' grizzly took it real personal like and came totally unglued. One minute I'm dozing in the saddle, the next I'm up to my ass in fur, blood, and kicking feet.

Hell hath no fury like a bear gone nuts! I'm not sure what happened next, but I was jammed between my saddle and a big old stump with a dead horse on top of me. There was blood all over the place and I could smell the breath of that bear. I was too scared to be hurt at the moment but I couldn't do a thing pinned the way I was. I hated to see that horse die but I was glad to see that bear hauling him up the bank and away from me.

I had to get the hell away from here. My rifle was in the saddle boot, so I had no chance if he came back for me. I rolled off the stump so I could crawl away into the brush. I think I screamed before I fainted.

● CHAPTER 2

Where lies the difference between consciousness and the subconscious? They say a drowning man's life will flash before his eyes; an omen of death? Or maybe just his mind, reaching out to hang on to something warm and decent, the subconscious taking over to help cloud the pain and sorrow of reality. I don't know, but my mind keeps slipping back and forth. One moment raging pain, the next blackness and nothing. And yet it seems I can hear horses cropping grass, I smell bread baking, and a voice singing softly, a song from long, long ago. A woman's voice, soft and sweet, the song a woman might sing in her kitchen, happy in her work.

Memories of long ago, or living my life over? God, it's so real. I ain't never been no believer and I don't know about now, but my senses have never been sharper. Like when I'm conscious it's the feeling of intense pain, but more than that, I can smell all the dampness and decay of the earth. I can hear the smallest of sounds like a whole chorus. The forest is alive with sound, fantastic. Even the grey of the sky and the colour of the trees have never been sharper than right now. A man gets carried away with life sometimes and can't see the forest for the trees. Ordinary sounds and colour just seem to blend in and you only notice the unnatural.

I'd put up my whole ranch for a drink of water right now. There's a canteen on that slope, under what's left of my horse, along with a bit of grub in my saddle bags, but it ain't doin' me a damn bit of good down here, and I can't move, not even a finger. I can move my head a little but that hurts like hell when I do, my back is broke I guess. I keep thinking of the damndest things I've done in my life, like when I got tangled up with Jake

Meers, and some of the stunts we pulled off, the things we did and the places we went, totally insane. I can remember him sittin' up all night nursing a sick cow than the next day he'd head straight for town and raise hell for two or three days and never think of his farm. A hell of a good guy but notional as all get out. No telling what he would dream up next.

I recall the last time we were together about eight, ten years back now. It was spring branding time and as usual I'd go help him, then, if he'd remember, he'd come help me. In those days he was running about three hundred head. I had about thirty five or so. Jake's always got done first. But this would be the last time I'd help him. Ol' Jake and I had spent three long hard days gathering, and sorting, and about noon of the fourth day we finished branding and castrating the last of those rotten critters. Now a few days ago we had figured them as a bunch of cute little critters, something nice to see. But right now they were just rotten critters, and I for one had seen enough of them to last me another season. Trouble was, I still had mine to do. Oh well, what the hell.

We headed on up to the house for dinner and Jake pulls down a jug of whiskey, says "Wes! Let's tie one on boy."

"Shit" I say, "Why not?" That brought a look from Gladys, his wife that would peel paint off an outhouse. I guess a man could use a wife but damn to be stuck with one like that. Reminds a man to steer clear of that sort of thing.

However, a crock of rye later and we're headed for town, gonna do it up right, yes sir. All of a sudden Jake gets the idea he needs a new pick up so we stop at the local Ford dealer and started kicking tires on a new four by four. I figure buying a new truck should keep us out of jail, as that's where we usually end up when we take on the town, it would be nice to go home with my money intact for a change. Good idea, Jake! Let's buy a truck.

Well we talked the sales man into putting a plate on it and would you believe it, that guy lets us take that truck on a test drive. Two half pissed cowboys covered in cow shit to their waist. What an idiot. Well sir, we went down one road and up another and at the edge of town where the creek flows under the road, Jake pulls her down over the bank and up the creek we go fasts as we can, rocks rattling off the bottom, mud flying everywhere. About half a mile of this and up the bank we go right through the middle of somebody's lawn. Was that guy pissed off or what. Wanted to know what in hell we think we're doing. Jake never bats an eye, just asks where the likker store is.

Well I gotta tell you it sure got interesting when we finally got back to the dealership and hour after they usually close. The sales manager came out and when he seen that truck he came completely unglued. Oh man the guy went nuts. Was gonna have us hauled off to jail and all sorts of things. jeez, there goes my cows and money again. It didn't help much either when Jake told the guy he should drop the price of the truck cause of the awful shape it was in, all banged up and dirty like. I thought the guy was gonna have a seizure of some sort.

Thankfully Jake bought the truck and at a reasonable price considering the whole situation. Going to town with Jake could be like sitting on a powder keg; you just never knew when it would blow in your lap. Wonder how Gladys will take this? Glad it ain't me what's gotta live with her. Although the ones I usually wake up with ain't much to brag about. Damn, I'm always scared I'll get completely pissed one night and invite one home to live with me.

It was two days later Gladys came and bailed us out, and we

headed for home. I swear the hell I'm not gonna hang around that guy no more. Something tells me Gladys is gonna love that.

God the pain is terrible. I gotta be delirious or something, I haven't thought of Jake in years. Hell of it is, I can't move. Right between my shoulders is on fire, no feeling in my fingers or toes. I'm in trouble I think, I hope Krista's OK. God, there's a girl if I ever seen one. Gonna make some guy a hell of a wife one day. Gutsy as they come. I remember the day she came to live with me, my brother was killed in a car accident and his wife went to pieces, wasn't able to look after herself let alone a twelve year old girl. Didn't take her long to settle in though. In two short years she came to running that place like she was born to it. Actually it was kind of nice coming home to a hot meal and a clean house for a change. A fellow gets to batching it and things kinda get let go after a bit. She was a real Godsend. Kind of helped settle me down a little.

It was getting to a point where every time I'd go to town I'd either end up cooling my heels in jail or some honky tonk angel was taking me for my money any way she could. Always amazed me a closing time how many real gorgeous women were wandering around that the other guys had missed. Unbelievable. When you're a big ol' raw boned guy like me it's kinda tough to get the pretty and quiet ones to pay you much attention, besides, they're the ones that get you into the most trouble anyway.

But how the hell I'll get out of this one I don't know. It's getting dark and I can hear something sniffing around out there. jeez, it won't be long now, the bears and coyotes and such will be down here, that horse smells to high heaven. I'll be in real trouble then, can't get my gun or a fire going. Kristen, I hope you're okay kid, I'm gonna be a while getting home, girl.

● CHAPTER 3

I guess life had never been no bed of roses for Mrs. Morgan's boy so I guess I'll go out the hard way if I have to. My dad and I were some of the first people in this country. I was a boy about nine years old, Mom passed on the year before and things just kinda went bad for Dad after that. Just home from the war, there was a drought, no work, and things were going real bad on the rented farm he had in Saskatchewan, so Dad sold what we didn't need, which wasn't much. My sister and brother were just babies so dad left them with my aunt until such time he could send for them and then we headed west with a wagon and team of Clydesdales that were Dad's pride and joy. It would be many years before I would see my brother again, my sister, never.

We packed some tools and equipment we'd need; a cross cut and swede saw, a couple of axes, a plow, and an anvil, and a 35 Winchester which I still have to this day. Can't buy shells for it anymore so it hangs above the door on a set of antlers, from a deer that I shot while I was drinking coffee on my veranda. My dad taught me to shoot with that rifle, he never missed. They taught him real good in the army and he passed it on to me. Dad never treated me like no kid, and included me in just about everything, including a little pull from the jug now and then. Not that he was a heavy drinker but we enjoyed the unusual benefits from time to time. I never seen the ol' man drunk though. He used to tell me "Wes, a man has to be responsible for himself and his actions at all times I never forgot that. Many times over the years I'd go out on a tear and cut my wolf loose as they say, but I never went looking for trouble although I must admit I never sent anyone home empty handed when he come lookin' for it. When it come to fightin' it was usually root hog or die. I won lots and lost some, my nose been broke a time or two, a scar across my wrist from a broken glass, and a dozen stitches on my cheek from a knife. That one made me mad and when thy broke that one up they hauled me to jail and him to the hospital with a broken arm and crushed hand. Using a knife! That's real chicken shit.

It took Dad and I most of three months to make it across country to settle in B.C.'s Peace River country. It took us awhile with that wagon. Dad was in no hurry and we looked the country over as we camped out along the way. Dad was real handy and we stopped here and there and had many a good meal with folks who set us up to dinner. We'd shoe horses, cut wood, fix harness, and at one point spent a week with a threshing crew. That was tough work but it was fun working with the men, some of them resented me as I was just a boy, but the old man set them straight real quick and I'd try that much harder just to prove myself for him. When we pulled into this town we camped on the edge of it for about two weeks and Dad went to work helping to build a house, I tended stock and cooked, and ran errands for whatever I could make. Ten days of hard work and the house was finished and we had some cash money, something kind of scarce at the time and was gonna help this winter. It was already late September and folks was wondering why I wasn't in school yet. I wasn't in no hurry and as long as the ol' man didn't bring it up I wasn't gonna. We settled on a piece of land about eight miles east of town along side a river, it was getting cold and heavy frost every night with a hint of snow in the air and us with no cabin yet. We rigged up a lean to to store our rigging' and we slept under the wagon, piling on all the tarps and cloths we could find to keep off the cold.

Now it's easy to say you can throw up a log cabin, and that's what we did but don't get the idea it's easy. First you have to cut the trees and pull the stumps then level the site, then you gotta peel the logs, notch them and trim them to fit tight, selecting only the ones that match up close enough to size. Then you gotta put some of those logs on a rig so you can cut planks for flooring and such. I got to go on top, which was hard 'cause you had to balance yourself and pull up on the heavy saw, but I felt sorry for the ol' man standing on the ground, all the dirt and sawdust running down on him steady in his shirt and hair and eyes, but I never heard him bitch. Not once. In fact for the first time in a year there was a glint in his eye, he was smilin' and crackin' jokes. It was great. We were more like partners than father and son.

That first year was hard, but hell, we knew no other way. Like I said, my dad was handy and that cabin showed it, we built small and snug, easy to heat, easy to look after. Twenty four by twenty four, two bedrooms and a general living area. Six foot walls, no ceiling. Dad salvaged two windows and a door off an abandoned house that was falling in. It wasn't much but we were proud.

I worked the rest of the winter in town at the general store and took my wages in a cookstove. I stayed right there with those people cause there was no way in and out. Everyday I worked seven in the morning to eight at night, six days a week. But Sunday Dad would come to town and see me and we'd walk and visit or go to someone's house for the day. Pop made friends easy and I knew everyone from the store so we were always welcome.

I quit the store in the spring, I was glad to be shut of the place. I'd had enough of stocking shelves and pricing doo-dahs to last me a lifetime. I enjoyed some of the customers and the way they treated me like a grown up and all, including me in conversations and the light hearted teasing they gave me, especially when I'd get goo-goo eyed over some pretty girl or another. But I was glad when Dad came and got me and took me home. Six months work for a cook stove, two boxes of shells, a pair of boots, and one sack of flour. There was a lot of people would gladly have done it.

That summer was hard work, sun up to sun down. And in this country daylight's about four a.m. to eleven p.m. from about May to August. But there was so much to do. We put up forty acres of wheat, plowed up, planted and cultivated with that team of Clydes. We built a small barn and fenced about sixty acres of bush pasture. Dad had kept busy all winter cutting and peeling logs and firewood. He had sold some furs so we were in reasonably good shape for the time. We cooked most of our meals outside as it was too hot in the house; fact is we slept out on the veranda as well. It was a hot summer and our wheat was coming real good. I traded two weeks of my time for six wiener pigs with our neighbour. Things were looking real prosperous.

That winter Dad and I took a contract cutting ties for the railroad and we made enough to buy seed and five bred heifers. We had a mild winter with lots of snow, so the going was slow but reasonably good. Dad was falling and trimming and I was skidding them out to the landing with the horses, where we'd cut them into ties. The railroad men would pick them up from there. Working outside all winter was great and I loved every minute of it, although I'd usually fall asleep on the horse's back before we'd get home at night. Dad would pack me in the house, do the chores then wake me up for supper. At eleven years old I didn't have much stamina yet.

The next year didn't go so well for us, we ate and got by but it was tough times. It snowed in June then it rained all summer and September dumped a heavy load of snow that stayed on. So we didn't get a crop off. I swear we shovelled a million feet of snow so the animals could eat the crop and get around. We lost two cows and one of my sows ate her young so we had to get rid of her. We needed the bacon and hams though. Dad took real sick in March and never really got better; pneumonia or something. He died that spring, he was out plowing and the wind got at him and he got sick again. He lasted about a week then one morning I brought him coffee and he was gone. For the first time in four years I cried.

I spent a long time disillusioned and the county came and hauled me to town. Put me in a foster home where I had to go to school. I made the most of it but all I did was go through the motions. I hated all of it. I was real trouble for the folks who had me, they tried to be decent to me but I wanted to go home to the farm and raise myself.

The County sold our animals at an auction and gave the money to my foster folks I guess, cause I never seen any of it and that made me mad. I worked hard beside Pop and I figured it was stolen from me, but no one was listening to twelve year old boy, so I beat the hell out of the police chief's son. I guess if they wouldn't pay me no mind I make them. When that boy crawled home they sure paid attention right away, not exactly what I had in mind, but I was too mad to care either.

The kid was two years older than me but never done no work in his life. I hurt him real bad. My foster folks didn't want no more of me so when I heard them speak of juvenile hall I cut and run. I was big for my age and passed easy for fifteen so no one bothered me, and I spent the next five years roaming around working at this and that. I worked threshing crews, farm hand, tried logging but I couldn't stay at anything. I wanted to go home to the farm but I was scared to. When I was seventeen I hired on with a drilling rig and I spent three years with them. It was good work and I learned fast and made it up to tool push, a top hand what more could a guy want. Just a farm I guess. Somewhere along the way the hate and fear had left me and I drifted back home. Course the farm was occupied by someone else by this time so I took homesteading rights on my first quarter section here on Buffalo Creek.

A lot of water goes under the bridge and time has a way of getting away on a man, when I look back on it I wonder would I do it different if I could? I guess not. It would be nice to have a son maybe to hand the ranch over to. Sort of make a man smile, trying to picture me old and wrinkled sittin on the porch, giving him a hard time, telling him how we did it in the good ol days. I could laugh if it didn't hurt so bad.

Shit, no need worrying about that, I'd be lucky to make it till daylight let alone worrying about sons and stuff.

I wish whatever was over there sniffing around would bugger off. It was kind of creepy knowing it would be over here working me over in a while, feeding off me, and not a damn thing I could do about it. God, Krista, don't hold supper sweetheart, I'm gonna be a tad late.

● CHAPTER 4

It's getting dark. Dark and cold, no stars and a feel of snow. Ain't no one ever gonna find me down here in this wash even if Rebel does find his way home, it will take him a couple days anyway. I know in the movies the horse always finds his way home fast and brings back help, but in real life a horse will stop and browse and amble on just sort of wandering. Sure they find their way home, but not straight out. Rebel probably ran a straight line till he tuckered out and settled down and likely would be tomorrow before he'd get oriented and find his way home. If it starts snowing they'll never track him back here. A hell of a way to cash in but sure beats laying in a bed or saddle bound to a wheel chair. No life for this cowboy.

Well I was leavin' no family behind except Kris. I never did marry, thought about it some, but rough lookin' beat up old boys like me don't get glance one from the kind of girl I'd want. Granted I'm no monk, but the ladies that occupy my time are a little too tough on the eyes and pocket book to want to look at them past sunup. It's amazing at midnight there's dozen of lovely ladies just waitin' for me to take them home and just as amazin' when I wake up in the morning and have to sneak out of their place so I don't have to see them awake. It's enough to scare me off booze and my wicked ways for at least a week or so, until my memory dims and Mother Nature gets me headed back to town with lust in my mind and sin in my heart.

When I settled that land fifteen years ago it set me back forty five hundred dollars, all the money I had to show for kicking around the country for all those years. I had enough to pay for the land, a horse and ten head of cattle. Things was lookin' kind of good for Mrs. Morgan's number one son. About then my ten cows were all in calf and I was counting my good fortune while splitting rails for fences and making improvements on the place. I rigged a lean to up of poles and canvas to keep my riggin' dry and a place in back so I could sleep out of the rain. I never minded much what kind of weather I worked out in. Mamma always said I never had sense enough to come in out of the rain but what I lacked in brains I made up for in enthusiasm, ingenuity and a strong back. You spend all your days cutting wood, putting up hay, breaking horses and working cattle, you're gonna have a hell of a time keeping meat on your bones and that's a fact.

I ain't bitchin', I wouldn't trade it for nothing else. But none of that was doing me any good right now. I can't feel the pain anymore just numbness and the cold and worse yet the wet touch of snow on my cheek, those big heavy ones that come down straight and slow and pile up fast. I'm glad the horse ain't suffering none.

It's times like this a guy gets to wondering if he should have taken up another way of life, like those town folks who do their eight hours then go home. Why just think of it, I might be sitting back right now sippin' whisky and watching the TV or something. It would beat the shit out of this right now and that's a mortal fact. I have no idea what time it is. I never carried a watch. Sooner eat when I'm hungry and sleep when I'm tired. There was always enough work to take care of the rest of it. I been conscious and unconscious so much I'm not sure of anything. Except maybe it's better when I'm out. I keep dreamin' of the good times and friends along the way. If it keeps up this snow I'll be buried under a foot or so of it by morning. Well I never begged to come on this ol' Earth. I guess it won't do much good to beg to stay. Screw it darling, we'll go dancing tomorrow night.

Have you ever bought a horse? Buying horses has got to be a fever. I've seen grown men, myself included, spend days roaming the country burning up gasoline and ignoring everything else including wives and families, just cause the horse buying itch has struck him. Now hunting down horses is an art. Contrary to what many folks say. Why you can spend days just roaming the country side chasing down one lead after another, the horse you find will be either too tall or too short or not right in the withers or maybe the pastern and maybe and most likely just too dam much money. It was no different when I went looking for that sorrel lyin' dead up there on the hill. Ol' Doc and I went cruising down one back road after another, sippin' on beer and telling tales of bad horses, mean cows, and the likes while keeping an eye out for something just right; something out of the ordinary. Hey this can be fun. You meet a pile of people like you just wouldn't believe, like one afternoon I spy an appaloosa in a corral that looked good. Pull her in here Doc! I said, we'll take a look. Now like I said, there's some real sights in this country and some such as this one would knock you right on your ass. I'm here to tell you that horse was the best looking thing on the place.

The old frame shack was sitting amongst junk and weeds piled up from one end of the yard to the other with every piece of crap imaginable. On the door step stood a woman big enough to burn diesel and mean enough to carry her own tanks, honest she stood well over six feet and had to go three hundred pounds. A face what looked like it was chiselled out of rock. She invites us up to the porch to chat, well she was no way gonna sell that horse but we may as well have coffee, what the hell! Why not. When I say that was a sorry outfit I mean it. The paint was all peeled, there was cardboard in a couple of window

panes and with the door open it smelled like a wolf's den even
out on the porch. So while we drank coffee that would burn
the guts out of a buzzard from cups that were dirty enough to
come when you called them, this woman tells us how she wid-
owed and been running this spread by her ownself for nigh on
five years. Man!She had a voice would rip nails from a tin roof.
Wow! Well sir being the friendly sort of man I am I start to hint
around how Ol' Doc here is a first rate farmer and bachelor to
boot and I tell her how he's been pinin' for just the right lady
to come along and rescue him from his rowdy ways. Why look
at him, Ma'm, I says, he just too shy to speak out his own self.
Yes siree Bob, you'd make a hell of a team. A woman could do
a lot worse you know. Man if you could have seen Doc's face. I
thought he was gonna have a shit haemorrhage or something.
I laughed so hard I thought I was gonna puke. Doc was so mad
he wouldn't talk to me for weeks. He bitched and fumed all the
way to town. Vowed he'd never help me with anything ever
again and I wasn't even to ask. Wanted to know what kind of
asshole I was anyhow. jeez, try to be nice and some folks just
don't appreciate it.

I had to find that little sorrel all by my own self; had to do it
the hard way. Went to the auction; ain't no fun in that at all.

I shouldn't leave a person thinkin' bad about ol' Doc 'cause
they sure don't come much better when it comes to knowing
horse flesh. Maybe three of four top hands that I know of and
he's definitely one of them. Break them out gentle and right is
what he does, when he was done you had a first rate cow pony
on your hands. Doc and I go back a few years and that's for
sure. The year I came home before I went on the rigs we spent
a winter breakin' a bunch of draft horses for Jim Meeker. All
registered stock. I was eighteen that year. I learned more about

horses that winter than most guys get to know in a life time.

Now lots of guys can break horses with ropes and guts and lots of cussin' and just what ever it takes, well that's OK I guess, so long as I don't have to own it. No you gotta take them one critter at a time, approach them like individuals 'cause that's just about what they are. There's as many personalities in horses as there is in humans; that is to say they're just like people; each one has to be handled different.

That winter we holed up in a cabin in Lost Valley, a few miles out of town, two miles of frozen wheel ruts that passes for a road off the main gravel one. This road's passable when it's bone dry or froze over which in this country accounts for about sixty percent of the time. Seems like it's snow to your neck or mud to your ass or visa versa each year different. That valley makes up about six hundred acres or better with some nice natural meadows and small creek running through the centre of it, neither of which was doing us any good at this point 'cause the creek was froze over, and this was the year for snow to our ass. What it boiled down to was an hour's worth of chores that took more like two hours or more every morning and night, leaving us about six hours of daylight to tackle the job at hand. Between cutting wood, chopping ice off the pond, melting snow for house water, a fellow didn't need to worry about getting bored. We were putting in twelve to fourteen hours every day working by lantern light much of the time.

Thankfully the cabin was snug and a decent stock of flour, sugar, coffee, and beans, but any meat we had we shot ourselves. There was more game around than you could handle at first. There was moose, deer, bear, elk and rabbits galore. The best part of the deal was when Doc would say, Wes! You best fetch meat boy. That meant a day of walkin' or riding up through those hills and looking over the country. Something I never tired of. Now I admit there's been a time or two I had to put a second shot in to finish a kill but I never missed what I shot at, never. Dad taught me better.

It was on one such morning I pulled out just before daylight. It was colder than usual and if I knew then, what I would later I would have stayed in bed, but such is the way of life and another lesson was to be taught by Mother Nature and she runs a harsh school. Only the tough survive and I damn near didn't. The day before there had been sun dogs and the weather had dropped about ten degrees or better but it wasn't that bad at the time, but as I went further and further back I started to worry, no birds were singing, the sun was hanging like a brass ball in a leaden sky. No sound except the crunching of the horse's feet as trees popped it echoed like a cannon in the frozen stillness. It was worse among the trees. There was no wind, just increasing cold. Nothing was moving so I turned for home. I was in an area I had never hunted before so it took me a while to get my bearings and when I topped out on what I called Flat Top Mesa I was about twelve miles from home. It was coming on dark and I wasn't prepared to overnight it. I could make do but it was gonna be rough. Getting a fire going was gonna be wild. Now, there's folks who claim they can get a fire started anytime, anyplace. Brother, try it with frozen bark and twigs when it's forty below or better. I finally managed it. It wasn't much comfort but the horses seemed to like it. So when the moon got up and thank God it was nearly full, the air cleared of ice fog and I want to tell you the sky was filled with a million stars.

Hey, that's pretty, but it was also well below forty degrees minus and there's was no way I could keep from freezing up so we lit out, me walkin' and leading the horse. Cold air like that is tough on the lungs and you gotta be careful; even a slight amount of sweat and you're gonna freeze to death. You have to move slow and steady stopping and doing the teamsters warm up once in a while. My feet were frozen, so were my hands. It took all night but we made it. When I came through the door Doc was making coffee, all he said was you picked a poor time to take a day of and go visiting.

Doc looked after my horse while I crawled into bed and died. I slept through the worst of it thankfully and when I awoke the burning and pins and needles were pretty well gone. It was near dusk and I realized how lucky I had been. It took three days for the swelling to go down enough for me to move around. My feet had swollen to twice their size, my nose looked like a light bulb, and my left hand was swollen up on the outside and felt like a ham, not to mention my ears. I looked like Hubert the Elephant. I looked pretty weird but it hurt too much to laugh. Doc made up for it though; more smart assed remarks than a stand up comic.

Shut up you asshole, I says. You brood around here, never say more than two words in as many weeks most time, so why start now?

I swear to God that's about the only time I seen Doc laugh.

I was very fortunate though and in a week or so everything was back to normal, I could have lost an ear or something. Although I've always been a little more sensitive to the cold since, it was a small price to pay.

● CHAPTER FIVE

I've worked at a lot of things over the years. Slashing crews, oil rigs, farm hand, stock handler, and I've enjoyed some and hated some and mostly indifferent unless I was working for myself. It's been said I'd tackle Hell with a bucket of water on my own time, but you couldn't pay me to do it. But a man's gotta eat so I gave a day's work for a day's pay. Even with the ranch, I would take on a small job for extra cash now and then if I could get away. One time I drove pilot car, hauling an oversized trailer to Whitehorse. That was a job I didn't care much for. You had to take your time leading the truck through the bends and bridges and such, only to have to drive all the way back again, but it paid not bad.

Actually we hauled this outfit through to Beaver Creek, took us four days. You could only run daylight hours, that's not much in November but the trip up was fairly uneventful, light snow, no winds and icy only in the shaded spots. But coming home was another story. In that country the weather can change in an hour. I've seen forty below at supper then have it go up and have water running in four or five hours. It can be real scary so your go prepared and only fools and new comers predict the weather. It was down by Johnson's Crossing that the wind picked up and it started freezing rain. She got so slick I decided to stop over at Teslin. I called down to the owners and got layover clearance. Hell I was stopping with or without it but Momma always said be polite, so I called. It was freezin' rain right through to Fort St John and getting worse.

Well that was quite an ordeal, I met a couple of truckers who had a bottle of whisky each and about eleven the waitress shut it down and joined us at the table. We played cards and danced to the jukebox until the morning shift came in to open up. They were real nice people, and it was two days before we could pull out again.

The rest of the trip was uneventful and I was home two days later. What a guy will go through to earn himself a few dollars, my, my.

Now don't get the idea my life's been one big adventure after another. I've had my share and you will when your lifestyle is such as mine, and there's many more like me, when you take each day as it comes, doing what you have to, tackling each problem head on and the devil take the hind site. As the saying goes "Give her hell and never look back." It's been a good life.

I know there's folks who work hard eight hours a day, five and six days a week for the same outfit. Cuddle up in their homes at night and watch TV with their families and short of two weeks camping or maybe a weekend hunting, life is pretty routine. But for us that have to live each day to the hilt, life is just one big challenge to be met head on and do the best we can with what we got.

All though it don't always seem much like adventure when your spending ten or twelve hours a day in the saddle or busting your back pounding fence posts, branding cattle or putting up hay in the blistering heat.

Try moving a herd of cattle from one bush choked pasture to another when they don't want to go all by yourself; there's one critter more stubborn than most women I ever met. A good cow pony sure helps, and if you got a good dog, then you got it made.

All you have to do is lose a couple of calves to wolves or bear or freak snow storms. It's enough to make you wanna cry. But you don't, you just stay at it and make what gains you can and hope it evens out in the end.

I've read stories of guys that struck it rich but not me, I worked hard for all I had and that was usually enough as I'm not a needful man and could make most anything or at least fix it. A high time for me was a day off, a cold beer, maybe go fishin. Not necessarily in that order and anytime I could get all three together was real rare occasion.

Granted I never had to fight wild Indians, plow my fields with a rifle strapped to the handle, or as far as that goes pay no hydro bill. But I had my share of scrapes, between Idiots trying to steal my cows, or take my ranch away, and trying to knock my head off my shoulders the odd Saturday night.

The bank tried to take my ranch a time or two but I managed to hang on, and one night my dog started going nuts so I slip outside and way off in my pasture I see tail lights. So I grab my Winchester and high tail it along the fence line real quiet like and here's a couple of idiots got six of my cows on the back of a truck. Well I went nuts and shot the front tires so they couldn't get away then I fired a few shots in the air scaring the hell out of them. They ran off pretty quick, but I left those cows right where they were for the time.

Would you believe it those Jack ass's show up the next day with the Queen's Cowboys and some cock and bull story how they was lost and decided to pull off the road for the night, they were just walking over to my place when I started shooting up the place; wanted me arrested and thrown in jail. Well they charged me and I had them charged and those Mounties sure pulled through for me. They spent some time scouting around and found where they had loaded the cows, they also had stolen the truck from Saskatchewan and they were wanted there for various reasons.

Biggest problem was we had a sit in judge from Vancouver

and he wouldn't believe that I had done the only thing possible at the time. He wanted me put away, couldn't understand me not going to the neighbours three miles away to phone the police. One of those anti-gun crusaders. My lawyer had a hell of a job of it but he pulled through for me. Cost me five hundred dollars for his fee.

Shit, I should have let them take the cows. I lost three days, five hundred dollars, and a bear got one of the cows anyway. Talk about justice

Where, oh where does the time go? How did I let this happen, letting life slip by? There's so much I'd like to do yet. A man gets so caught up with what he's doing he sometimes forgets he's not here forever and it's as plain as the snow on my face that I've run my string out here and now, and there ain't no turnin' back the clock, that's a fact. I never realized how much I enjoyed life. It's taken me fifteen years to build the Diamond E into what it is today and I wanna tell you it's been hard summer and winter, heat, rain and cold. I was out there doing what needed done. The first year I didn't have a cabin at all. I built a lean to in the edge of the brush, just a pole tied between two trees with four or five more long heavy poles draped across the top pole and leaning down to the ground with a couple heavy canvases spread over the frame work. There was enough room for my gear, and me to sleep out of the rain. I had a small log barn built by late fall for the horses and I slept in the hay mow that winter. And yes there was many a night I was awake most of it keeping a fire goin' when the temperature dropped well below thirty degrees minus, but I was fortunate as the winter was fairly mild with one Chinook after another blowing in. One day you're working at thirty below with everything frozen solid, a couple days later you're slipping and sliding around in

the slush and muck where the cows had things stirred up. But I
made it through and in the spring I built a cabin. Be damned if I
was spending another winter like that! No way. The next winter
was so severe I lost two cows that were calving late in February.
When you only have a small herd that really hurts. It was four
years before I even ate beef. I lived on moose, deer, rabbit and
grouse. All good eating but it felt good when I could finally afford to eat a piece of beef. My first cabin, just a one room affair
about twelve feet by sixteen, was nothing but charred embers
one night when I come riding in from town. To this day I can't
figure out what caused that fire. It was early spring of my second year and most everything I owned was in that place. All I
had left was the clothes on my back, my rifle and saddle. Well
no cows or horses were hurt so it was start all over again. This
time I moved back into the lean to and taken my time and built
a home a little more substantial. Built it like a tee with the main
living room at the front and centre, a hall with two bedrooms
down one side, and a kitchen with a good pantry and butcher-
ing room down the other. Two years later my barn went up in
smoke and I lost two good mares in foal. I guess my hay was
too damp in the mow and it heated up. Like I said it took me
fifteen years and it still isn't all that much. I remember the fifth
winter I was there, the Kendahls moved in down the way and
it was lucky for me they did. It was just before Christmas and
I was trapping along the creek. I was maybe four or five miles
from home when I slipped on the ice and broke my arm and
bruised my hip so bad I thought I broke it too. Thankfully it
happened early in the morning; it took me all day to get back to
the house. Jim drove me into the doctor's the next day. My arm
never did set straight and has bothered me ever since

It was shortly after that my brother showed up. That was

really something. I'd pretty well forgotten about him and my sister, it had been so many years. He stayed on with me for better than a year then he met a girl from town and got himself hitched up. We built a cabin for them on the ranch but she was a complaining woman and had no use for farming, cows, or any of it. She wanted town and lights and neighbours and such. Krista was about the only good thing came of that. Certainly the best thing that happened to me, that's for sure. I couldn't love that girl more than if she was my own.

● CHAPTER SIX

Kristin waited a couple of days longer than the date marked on the calendar that hung beside the table. Her Uncle Wes couldn't keep track of time no matter what. To him seven days, or two weeks was all the same. But she was starting to worry, the last three days it had been snowing hard and drifting real bad. An early winter storm set in, the school had been closed today and she knew it would be worse higher up where her uncle was. She was not a panicky type and was not concerned about herself or the farm, the house was stocked well with food enough for two years if need be. It had been a good year for the farm. There was ample feed for the cattle; it was just a matter of keeping water holes open until calving time in early March. If there was trouble, Jim and Donna down the road would be right here. Taking her cup of coffee to the table she watched with enthusiasm as a speck appeared on the horizon slowly getting closer until she could distinguish a horse through the frost coated window; a horse with no rider. Grabbing her coat she ran through the door and for the first time in years she cried as she watched Rebel limp into the yard with the pack saddle hanging under him.

She didn't really remember stripping off the saddle or putting him into the barn or the fast ride to Uncle Jim's on Ranch Boy, her pinto pony.

While Donna settled Kristin down and got her a cup of coffee, Jim paced the floor. What the hell was he to do? It was snowing too hard to go racing off across country on a wild goose chase., You couldn't even find the tracks from Kristin's horse where she came down the driveway, let alone anything Rebel may have left; fat chance. Damn it all to hell anyway, he felt so useless. That Wes was in trouble was no doubt; there was no other reason he wasn't home and that horse was in the shape he was. Weather forecast was calling for another two or three days of this storm so it would be at least four or five days before he could start a search. He knew finding anything would be nearly impossible, but if Wes could move around at all he would be OK. He'd be holed up someplace high and dry with a fire going, he'd make out somehow. The man was one of the best there was in the bush but some how he felt uneasy. That horse wouldn't wander off. He was too well trained and Wes wouldn't send him home with the pack saddle. He would need that and the cuts and blood were not from traveling. He'd run up against a bear or a cat or something. It did not look good, and there was little doubt in his mind that his friend was in a bad spot. Kristan you stay here with Donna and I'll go up and look after things at the Ranch. We'll get a crew together and start a search as soon as possible. Nothing in Kristans life had been easy, her father, a construction worker had never been home for any length of time as work kept him away long hours and moving around the country from one project to the next was a way of life for them. The Diamond E was the only permanent home she had known in her life time. Her father had been killed in a car wreck, and her mother was in a care home, disabled. And couldn't even care for her self. Uncle Wes was her only family, and now he was missing. At sixteen Kristan looked more like eighteen, a serious child who excelled in school and had a keen interest in what was going on in the world. Although a good looking girl she didn't enjoy the popularity the other girls did at her age. Boys shied away from her, she was to sure of herself, and had away about her that made them nervous, and uneasy with her.

One thing she was sure of, No one was going to take here away from her home. She would stay and look after the farm until Uncle Wes was found no matter how long it took When he got home every thing would be as good as when he left. Three days later mounted on Snow mobiles Jim Kendahl with a Mountie and two others left the Diamond E yard with supplies for three days. There were no tracks to follow, but Jim knew how Wes thought and had good knowledge of the country they had to travel, but there was forty five miles give or take to where Wes had been camping and it was a lot of country under a pile of snow. A formidable task that had to be done, even knowing it would most likely be useless. It was a sad group of people who sat around the kitchen table the night of there return.

All that could be done, had been and there was not a lot left to say. They would make another try in the spring if Wes didn't show up by then, and every one knew that wasn't likely.

● CHAPTER SEVEN

It's snowing hard now, but I don't feel anything. No hunger, or thirst, no pain. Everything's OK. I don't regret my life. In a way I'm kinda proud. I was never a church going man, and I'm not sure about meeting my maker as they say, but I have to admit it's been great. Like sitting a horse on a brisk fall morning gazing down off a ridge through the trees, showing off their colourful coats. Watching the steam from the noses of the cattle as they graze on the frost covered grass. The sky a washed out blue and the air filled with the honking of the geese as they start their long trek southward. Oh, how I want to do that one more time.

I feel proud Kristin turned out to be the fine young lady she's become. Good at her studies, learning a good, quiet way of life that goes back a long, long time; like baking and cooking or keeping a good home, something that brings her satisfaction of a job well done. She'll make someone a hell of a wife, the kind to walk tall beside a man as a partner, not a dull person who follows along and holds a man back.

Team work is the only answer or else you never get anywhere, you just run around in circles, getting nowhere.

I wish I had showed her my little hidey hole in the root cellar, there's a letter there she may need leaving the ranch and all to her, and there's five hundred dollars cash tucked away for emergencies. I didn't think she'd have to worry about that just yet, so I never was in a hurry to show her. No one else knows either. Damn it! I taught her to ride and rope, she learned how to pull a calf, how to spot and treat ring worm and pink eye. She could shoot rifle or shot gun along with the best of them, I should have told her about that too.

Well there was no money owing on the place, everything was paid for. The cabin was well stocked for winter and as long as some big nosed Government man didn't come snoopin' around she'd be alright. She had a head on her shoulders. Now you might think a fifteen or sixteen year old can't manage on their own, well you're probably right in most cases, but there were exceptions and this sure as Hell was one of them. She had a head on her shoulders, and where we live, out on the Diamond E, we got no hydro. We have a radio phone that works most of the time and our nearest neighbours are three miles away. The bus turns around in our driveway so getting to school's no problem as long as the road's open. Trouble is I never taught her how to worry and in a couple days or so, she's gonna go out of her mind. She'll go to Kendahl's place; a good neighbour with wife and family of his own to worry about. I know he'll organize a search right away but he's gonna have to be a blood hound to find me way down in here covered over with snow like I am. But he'll try and what's more important they will help Kristin all they can. He knows what that place means to her and how much I'd want her to have it. Jim will know I've got a hidy hole somewheres on the property so maybe he will think to look for it.

It pays to have good neighbours; this country was full of them, helping each other out along the way. Why just start to build a barn or something and out of nowhere here they come; giving you a hand with this and that, when ever they could. You should see what happens when a family gets burned out. Why in a few days there's a dance social, we take the family into our homes and help them get back on their feet again anyway we can. They say the times are changing; but I hope this is one way of life that remains untouched here.

Jim Kendahl and I have shared a lot over the years he's been my neighbour. Together we own a baler and a stooker, a three ton truck, a couple of tractors and other equipment. Some I bought, some he bought, and some we pooled. What we had we shared, and if I couldn't fix it or run it, he could. It was a good situation. We never fought if we both needed it; we just helped each other until the job was done.

Jim had a section of land and was running Herefords, and putting up hay. He also had a bit of a logging show going on, and cut rough lumber for folks, mostly one by six and two by fours or six by six timbers. He did alright for himself.

● CHAPTER 8

Sam Cookson and Billy Waters had signed on the payroll for Can Am Western. They were part of a slashing crew. On this particular day they were cleaning up a survey line down in a gully in Willow Valley. A rambunctious pair of local boys, they were trying to outdo each other, this was Friday and the loser would have to stand for the beer this weekend.

"Billy" Sam said, "are you ever gonna settle down and marry that Morgan girl or what? You been spending more time trying to tie that filly down this past year than it would take to marry half of the women in this country. What do you see in her anyway? She's rougher than most guys I know. She's as pretty as they come, but boy you step out of line and I swear she'll throw you, hog tie you and brand your ass with that Diamond E like she does those calves each spring."

"Oh, Hell, Sam I know. But there's a girl would charge hell

with a snow ball for you if you treat her right. Any woman who
can hold down a spread like that is just the woman for me. I'll
never tame her, Sam. But what a partner she's gonna make, and
that's what I want, a partner, not some girl that's gonna drive
me nuts, and keep me broke wanting all the frivolous things
and too damn lazy or scared to go out and help or get a little
cow shit on her boots!"

"Did they ever find the deed or the will to that place Bill? You
know it must be eight or nine years since Wes disappeared, I still
can't figure that one out you know. If the story I heard is right
that guy was supposed to own everything outright, and there
should be money stashed all over the place in hidden places. He
hated banks 'cause they tried to take his place or something."

"Well Sam, my dad knew Wes good as anybody, they were
neighbours and friends for a lot of years. Dad's convinced
there's a deed and will stashed around in some well hidden
place but he could never find it. I don't think there's any money
though, or at least not enough to worry about. Kris has been
able to keep the place 'cause there's no money owing on it and
the bank showed documents to the court that Wes had signed
years ago for a loan or something that proved he owned the
land. Dad's been helping her where he can and the cow opera-
tion makes enough to keep things afloat. Jeez she's got to own
a couple hundred head of bred cows now, she's shrewd and has
built up the herd slow and easy, culling out the bad ones and
taking only small losses when she had to."

"Hell lets blow this joint Bill! It will be dark by the time we
get back to camp, and it's gonna snow sure as hell, an early
winter this year man! You bet."

A hundreds yards away, amongst the rocks and brush, in a
dry wash, what was left of a human skull stared, vacant eyed

across the rocks at the remains of a deer the wolves had taken some time ago. Neither one was much interested in whether it snowed or not. The rain, the wind, the elements had taken their toll long ago and nothing remained to keep Vigilent over the rest of the bones that lay strewn about. Remnants of other critters that had met the fickle hand of fate in this loneliest of places where no one ever came, except maybe the bears or wolves and such. Even they didn't stay.

People who have camped up in the area will tell you they hear the weirdest sound in the evening. Like a horse wandering aimlessly and a voice softly calling in the night. Of course it's probably just the wind or something as it brushes down through the trees and gently kisses the grass and plays among the rocks and the human skull that stares hollow eyed, watching as an eagle soars through the grey evening sky, flaunting his freedom and caring not, for he too had fed from time to time on the bones that lay below.

Song of the Wild

Who cries over the bones of those that lost there way
Who prays for the souls of those who've gone astray
The wind and the rain, have they taken there toll
Who mourns the loss of the wandering soul

Have they been called home has the master spoken
Is there a light at the gate to guide them in
Did the vultures and coyote each eat there fill
And scatter there bones to the rain and the wind

As evening shadow's fall across this land
And find us home both safe and sound
Think of the ones who just disappeared
And pray that their souls have been found

A.G. Wayne Ezeard (1986)